LET'S DO THIS!

Adapted by Alexa Young

Based on the series created by Michael Jacobs and April Kelly

Part One is based on the episode "Girl Meets Gravity," written by Randi Barnes.

Part Two is based on the episode "Girl Meets the Secret of Life," written by Mark Blutman.

DISNEP PRESS

Los Angeles · New York

Printed in the United States of America
First Edition, January 2016
1 3 5 7 9 10 8 6 4 2
Library of Congress Control Number: 2015938884
ISBN 978-1-4847-2813-0
FAC-025438-15324

For more Disney Press fun, visit www.disneybooks.com
Visit DisneyChannel.com

SUSTAINABLE
FORESTRY
INITIATIVE

Certified Chain of Custody
Promoting Sustainable Forestry

www.sfiprogram.org
SFI-01054

The SFI label applies to the text stock

PART ONE

CHAPTER 1

Riley Matthews was on top of the world. Literally. At least, she *looked* like she was somewhere out there, floating in space, the earth spinning beneath her feet, as she thought about how amazing her life was—how amazing it was to be alive, period.

"Riley Matthews," she said as planets spun behind her. "From Greenwich Village, New York City, the United States of America, continent of North America, Western Hemisphere, Earth, the solar system, the universe. The mind of God. And in the middle of all of it is John Quincy Adams Middle School. Me and my friends. Because we are the center of the universe. At least, that's what I thought. . . ."

Riley crashed back down to Earth. She was in her bedroom. In her bed. Nestled beneath her cozy purple comforter. And she didn't want to come out.

"Who's ready for a brand-new year?" Riley heard her mom, Topanga, say enthusiastically as she flung open Riley's bedroom door.

Ugh. Riley wasn't sure she was ready for her mom, let alone a brand-new year. She should have been excited about starting eighth grade, but there was one tiny detail weighing on her. Heavily.

"Why are you still in bed?" Mrs. Matthews asked.

Riley yanked the covers off her face.

"Is *he* gonna be my teacher?" she hissed at her mother.

"What? No! We are not doing that again. *That* was crazy!" Mrs. Matthews insisted. "New year. New teacher. Get excited, because you and your

4

friends are the kings of middle school now."

Riley began to smile, her heart filling up with hope. But then in walked her dad.

"First day of a new year!" he declared before noticing Riley was still under the covers. "Why are you still in bed?"

"Are *you* going to be my teacher?" Riley narrowed her eyes, the sight of him reviving all of her doubts.

"No!" Mr. Matthews shook his head. "Your mother and I went through that with Mr. Feeny."

"Yeah," Mrs. Matthews giggled. "He was our teacher from sixth grade to college."

They all shared a look of bewilderment. There was something very, very wrong about having the same teacher for that many years in a row. Riley thought about what life would be like if her *dad* was her teacher for that many years. Ick. Ack. *No.*

"How could that happen?" she asked them.

"In an unexpected—" Mr. Matthews began.

"But completely believable way—" Mrs. Matthews continued.

"Every year," Mr. Matthews concluded, shaking

his head again. Even he didn't quite seem to believe it had happened. That it *could* happen.

Before Riley had a chance to process the awful notion any further, Maya Hart appeared outside the bay window of Riley's bedroom. Maya was Riley's best friend in the whole wide world.

"What up, losers?" Maya said with a smile. In one swift move, she jumped through the window, kicked off her shoes, dove into bed next to Riley, and pulled the comforter up over both of their heads.

"No, no, no! No doing that, girls," Mr. Matthews warned as he jumped up onto the foot of the bed. "School!"

"Who's gonna be my teacher?" Maya asked, peeking out from beneath the covers.

"*Your* teacher?" Mr. Matthews asked. "Whoever loses."

Riley stared her father down. "I don't believe you," she told him.

"I'm telling you, girls. I'm gonna be teaching

your life to a whole new group of students," he insisted, jumping off the bed.

Riley turned to look at Maya. "Do *you* believe him?"

"I can't even believe we're starting the new year without first talking about how we were on the subway and you took Lucas by the face and—"

"Ah! Ha ha ha! We are *not* talking about that!" Riley kicked Maya onto the floor as she stood on top of her bed and victoriously flung out her arms, proclaiming, "We're kings!"

Riley was already dressed in the pink-and-gold top and matching skirt over denim leggings that she had carefully picked out for the first day of school. She jumped off the bed, headed straight for the bay window, and grabbed her backpack, eager to make her escape.

"We're kings, Matthews!" Maya cheered, skipping over to Mr. Matthews and getting right up in his face. "You don't get to tell us what to do anymore."

"Get out," Mr. Matthews told Maya, pointing to the window.

"Okay, but that was the last one," Maya said, waving a menacing finger at him.

Riley walked back to her father. "Dad, you have to let us learn to walk through life on our own two feet," she said. With that, she spun around and followed Maya out the window.

"Hmmm." Mrs. Matthews picked up one of Maya's zebra-striped ankle boots, both of which were still lying on Riley's bedroom floor. "You think they'll be back?"

"No, I think they're gonna go with this," Mr. Matthews replied, picking up one of Riley's spiky black boots.

Crazy as it seemed, Riley and Maya were indeed headed to school—each one walking on her own two *bare* feet—and Riley's parents could hear the sounds of the girls yelping in pain with each step they took away from the Matthewses' apartment.

"Ow," Riley said.

"Ow," Maya echoed.

"Ow." "Ow!" The girls' alternating voices could be heard as they made their way down the block.

They had to show Riley's parents—especially her dad—that they were prepared to endure a little pain if it meant a successful escape. They could only hope that said escape also included not having Mr. Matthews as their teacher again that year.

CHAPTER 2

Riley and Maya finally arrived at school. "Ow." "Ow!" The cries continued with each painful step. When they got to the landing at the top of the stairs overlooking the indoor quad, they stopped and smiled broadly at their loyal subjects—er, fellow students.

"Hellooo," Riley bellowed, stretching out her arm in a grand, sweeping gesture. "It is us. The kings!"

As Riley and Maya continued down the stairs and toward the history classroom, they ran into their friend Farkle.

"Hey, look at your feet," Farkle said, his eyes

widening with a bit too much excitement. "They're naked!"

"Eyes up here, buddy," Maya scolded.

"Hey, Riley, is your dad gonna be our teacher again this year?" Farkle asked while they walked through the quad.

"He said he's not," Riley replied.

"I'll believe it when I *don't* see it," Maya said.

As they neared their first-period classroom, Riley nearly bumped into Lucas Friar. Her heart felt like it might explode. She was excited to see him but also totally freaked out. In his blue-and-black-checkered button-down shirt, with his sparkling green eyes and perfectly spiky dark blond hair, he looked even cuter than usual. But ever since that day on the subway, things had become weird between them. Weirder than weird.

"Oh. Hi." Riley locked eyes with Lucas and tried to remain calm.

"Hey," Lucas replied slowly. "Hi. Hey."

"Hi," Riley repeated.

"All summer." Maya frowned with disgust.

"Hey," Lucas said again.

"You have to talk about it," Maya told them sternly.

"She's right, we—" Lucas began.

"Hi," Riley interrupted.

"Oh, hey," Lucas replied as the perfectly timed first-period warning bell rang.

"Glad we talked about it." Riley smiled up at Lucas.

"Yeah, me too," Lucas agreed.

"Bye," Riley said.

"Hey . . ." Lucas said as they all headed into class.

"Hey . . ." Farkle parroted to Maya, who could only roll her eyes at the entire situation.

But then, standing there in the doorway of the classroom, she closed her eyes completely. So did Riley. It was as if they were perched on the edge of a cliff, about to fall into the vast, terrifying unknown.

"I know it's gonna be my father," Riley said, shaking her head and swallowing hard.

"I can't look," Maya replied.

"Scared," Riley agreed, and they both placed their hands over their eyes. "Okay, ready?"

"Quick peek," Maya said. "One, two, three, go!"

The girls lowered their hands just enough to peer over at the teacher who was sitting casually on the edge of the desk at the front of the classroom. He glanced up from the folder he had in his hands. He wore a polished gray suit and purple tie and had skin like a caramel mochaccino. His dark brown eyes looked sweetly in the girls' direction. Not only was he cute, he *wasn't . . . Mr. . . . Matthews*!

Almost immediately, the girls both covered their eyes again.

"Did you see what I saw?" Riley asked, her heart racing with happy excitement this time.

"Oh, yeah," Maya said enthusiastically.

"Then why are we covering our eyes?"

"Because it's gonna go away and I don't want it to go away and it's gonna go away."

Finally, the girls uncovered their eyes and looked at the teacher again. Riley could hardly contain herself. Her eyes widened with amazement and her whole body began to shake.

"Yyyyyyyaaaaaaayyyyyyy!" Riley said, continuing to convulse as she exchanged giddy glances with Maya.

"Thank you," the teacher said with an awkward smile. "Girls, take a seat."

Riley and Maya rushed to the teacher's desk and cozied up next to him.

"*Your* seats," he clarified.

The girls headed to their usual desks in the front row and looked up at the teacher, putting on their most captivating smiles, eager to out-dazzle each other.

"Yeah, okay, let's get started," the teacher said, standing up and heading to the chalkboard. "Belgium. 1831."

"Yyyyyyyaaaaaaayyyyyyy!" Farkle's entire body began to shake in his seat, just likc Riley's had moments before, his eyes equally wide with excitement.

"This is gonna be our best year ever!" Riley

beamed as she turned to look at Maya, though she definitely wasn't talking about Belgium.

"Let's just get up and go over and look at him up close," Maya proposed.

The girls slowly rose from their desks and crept up to where their teacher stood at the front of the classroom. They examined him like lions stalking a wounded gazelle.

"Yes?" he asked.

"He said yes," Riley whispered.

"What do we do now?" Maya asked.

"I'm gonna touch him on the face," Riley replied, lifting her hand and slowly inching a burgundy-polished fingernail closer . . . closer . . . closer to the teacher's nose.

His eyes grew wider and wider as Riley's finger approached his face, until he finally lost his cool. "Sit down!" he commanded.

Riley and Maya dutifully obliged, turning around and taking their seats again.

"You two strike me as a couple of girls who are

used to special treatment," the teacher said sternly. "I don't know who your last teacher was, but I don't do that."

"Farkle time, sir?" Farkle interjected, raising his hand.

"Go ahead, kid," the teacher groaned. "You gotta farkle, you gotta farkle."

"No, this is where he takes over the class," Lucas attempted to explain, always the polite southern gentleman. It was one of his most swoon-worthy qualities.

"Oh." The teacher looked completely baffled. "He takes over the class? And you just talk without raising your hand? And these two just do whatever they want?"

Lucas raised his hand.

The teacher called on him. "Yes?"

"Pretty much, yeah," Lucas said with a shrug.

"You know what?" the teacher said, struggling to remain calm, his voice growing angrier with each word. "I wanted to make a difference. I wanted to shape young minds. I wanted to dedicate my entire life to being an influential person who commands respect!"

Riley got up from her desk, intent on examining this fascinating new teacher and his fascinating new way of teaching. She raised her hand to his face again, waving her finger all around, slowly stretching it out until—at long last—she placed it right on the tip of his nose.

"I quit!" The teacher threw up his hands in defeat, spun on his heel, and marched straight out the door.

What? NO! Riley's heart sank as she considered the gravity of what had just occurred. She sat down at her desk and turned to look at Maya. "What happens now?"

Maya widened her eyes at Riley and they both looked at the classroom door—hoping against hope that their new teacher was kidding. That he was just pretending to be upset with them. That he would come back. But no such luck. Instead, in walked the last person on the whole planet they wanted to see: Mr. Matthews.

He stormed straight over to Riley, pointed a finger in her face, and fumed, "*You* did this!"

So much for the best year ever.

CHAPTER 3

The whole situation was horrifying. Unbelievable. Unacceptable. "I can't believe you're going to be my father again!" Riley huffed at Mr. Matthews. His face contorted in confusion. "I said what I said," she added unapologetically.

"Okay." Mr. Matthews nodded, beginning to understand.

"Seriously, Matthews. How's this possibly happening?" Maya demanded.

"I like that it's happening," Farkle interjected. "That other guy wouldn't give me Farkle time."

"Yeah, he didn't like it at all when we talked," Lucas agreed.

"It's true," Maya said. "It was like *he* wanted to talk all the time."

Riley had to admit each of her friends had a point. "I don't think he knew that history class is supposed to be about *our* lives," she added.

Mr. Matthews's face relaxed into a slightly amused smile. "Galileo," he said, setting down his bag on the desk and taking his old familiar place in front of the chalkboard. "Everyone believed the sun revolved around the earth—except for him. Everyone thought that they were the center of the universe and that everything else circled around them."

"I know someone who circles around me," Riley chimed in. "A little too closely."

"Is that what you think is happening?" Mr. Matthews asked, walking over to Riley and then leaning against the front of his desk.

"We're in eighth grade now," Riley told him.

"We're a year older," Maya said.

"We should be able to head off and explore without you," Riley continued.

"Okay . . ." Mr. Matthews nodded. "And you guys think you're ready?"

"Born ready." Maya smiled, always the picture of cool confidence.

But Riley wasn't quite so sure about that one. "I'll get there!" she offered.

"Y'know what we're gonna do, Matthews?" Maya said. "We're gonna transfer outta here!"

"Yeah!" Riley agreed. Then, not exactly clear on what she was agreeing to, she turned to look at her best friend. "Yeah?"

"Yeah!" Maya nodded.

"Lucas? Farkle?" Riley asked, turning around in her chair. She was still feeling weird about things with Lucas, but she didn't want to go anywhere without the rest of her friends.

"I don't think so, Riley," Lucas replied.

Sigh.

Farkle shook his head in dissent, too. "I really like him."

"I like what he teaches us, and I like how we're talking right now and he doesn't stop us when he could if he wanted to," Lucas added before turning to Mr. Matthews. The whole class, somewhat confused, joined Lucas in a questioning look as he asked Mr. Matthews, "Why don't you stop us?"

Mr. Matthews smiled his tiny, somewhat annoying *I've got 'em now* smile. "Yeah, that's interesting, isn't it?"

"Well, we're done with you," Maya told him, pulling a dollar bill from the pocket of her green army jacket and smacking it into his hand as she shook it. "Thanks for the lessons. Buy yourself something pretty."

"Thank you." Mr. Matthews grinned, taking the money. "Oh—but you're gonna need transfer slips."

"I knew it," Maya groaned. "He's gonna keep us here on a technicality."

But before the girls could insist that he let them go, Mr. Matthews pulled out two green transfer slips and handed them to Riley and Maya without the slightest hint of sadness. "G'head. Beat it."

There was no way that just happened. It had to be a trick. Didn't it?

But Maya made it clear that it most definitely *had* happened.

"Look at us, Riles," Maya said, taking her slip and heading for the door with Riley and her own slip following right behind. "Two independent women, takin' their own road, makin' their own way with their guts and their brains!"

"Needin' nothin' from nobody from this moment on!" Riley joined in, turning to wave a finger at her dad and the class before walking out the door and slamming it behind her.

"Here comes funny," Mr. Matthews told the class as they looked at him, bewildered.

A moment later, Riley and Maya opened the classroom door just enough to each poke one bare foot inside. Right on cue, Mr. Matthews grabbed the girls' shoes from his bag and tossed them out the door into the hall, where the girls had retreated.

"Ow," Riley said.

"Ow," Maya echoed.

In that moment, Riley wasn't sure how to feel about what had happened with her dad. There was something comforting about his being there. She knew she still needed him. It was just a question of how much.

CHAPTER 4

Riley seemed to be floating through space again—not quite on top of the world, but somewhere out there.

"We think we're the center of the universe. We think everything revolves around us," she said as the sun rose behind her, lighting up the earth. It was magnificent. "We depend on the sun for light, for warmth. Every morning. Every day. And when it's gone, we sleep." As the sun's light disappeared back behind the earth, Riley added, "Trusting that in the morning it will always come back again."

Later that day, on the other side of town, Riley's mom and little brother walked into Svorski's Bakery. Mrs. Matthews had recently become part owner of the place. She did it to stop a major developer—represented by none other than her own law firm—from shutting it down. She couldn't let the place just disappear after all the years she and Mr. Matthews had spent there as kids.

"Auggie! Topanga!" Mrs. Svorski said in her thick eastern European accent.

"I'm dropping off your helper for the day," Mrs. Matthews replied brightly as Auggie sat down with Mrs. Svorski at a round table in the middle of the bakery.

"Oooh, good. Big, strong man," Mrs. Svorski replied.

"That's me!" Auggie beamed with pride.

"Mrs. Svorski used to attract all the big, strong men," the old woman told Auggie and his mom. "You know what happened?"

"What?" Mrs. Matthews asked.

"No, I'm asking!" Mrs. Svorski said with a mischievous smile.

Mrs. Matthews laughed, gave Auggie a big kiss, and started toward the door. But Mrs. Svorski stopped her before she could get very far. "Oh, Topanga, we need talk," she said. "You need to spend more time here."

"Well, Mrs. Svorski, how can I do that?" Mrs. Matthews asked.

"Mrs. Svorski, tell me the joke!" Auggie interrupted.

But the old woman continued to speak to Mrs. Matthews. "You quit shark lawyer job and you help turn this Old World place into place for young people."

"But this place has been here for so long," Mrs. Matthews said.

"*Too* long. Is creaky," said Mrs. Svorski, slowly rising from her chair and walking over to one of the weathered booths. "Is tired. Knows time is up. *Ding!*"

"How does a *bakery* know that its time is up?" Mrs. Matthews crossed her arms in front of her chest, unconvinced.

"It knows. You my partner. You bring new life. I need you here," Mrs. Svorski insisted, tapping her hand on the worn wood of the tabletop.

"Mrs. Svorski. Tell me the joke!" Auggie begged again, placing himself between the two women.

"Okay." Mrs. Svorski looked down at the curly-haired little boy as she sat in the booth. "Is not *U*-krainian bakery, is *my*-krainian bakery!"

Mrs. Svorski and Auggie both began to laugh but then stopped suddenly. "It's not funny anymore," Auggie said, frowning.

"I know," Mrs. Svorski replied. "You think I need little poochkie like you to tell me joke isn't funny? In old country I had variety show. It was called *Mrs. Svorski's Not-So-Happy Hour.*"

"Can you make the joke funny for me again?" Auggie asked, eyes wide and hopeful.

"Can *you* tell your mommy world is changing? Bakery must change, too."

Auggie turned and commanded, "Mommy, do it."

"But this place is so charming," Mrs. Matthews insisted, taking a seat across from Mrs. Svorski at the booth and leaning across the table to look into her eyes. "It's so . . . you."

"Yeah, people come, people go. Reminds me of song I sang at end of variety show." Mrs. Svorski smiled as she stood back up, lost in happy thought.

"Oh, here we go," Mrs. Matthews said, grinning.

"Make new friends and treat them nice," Mrs. Svorski sang, swaying her hips and snapping her fingers as she leaned over and stared down at Auggie. *"Because you never know who is spy!"*

Auggie's face fell, and he looked confused and slightly worried.

"Okay, how's this? I'm gonna spend a little more time here, and I'll also try to find someone to help you out," Mrs. Matthews proposed.

"Also you change name of place," Mrs. Svorski commanded.

"What?" Mrs. Matthews said. "No, this place will always be Svorski's."

"No such thing as always," the old woman insisted, sitting back down at the booth. "Now place Svorski's, soon place Topanga's. World keep turning. Life go to next people. This has always been good idea."

Mrs. Svorski smiled softly as Mrs. Matthews reached across the booth, taking both of her hands and squeezing them tightly. Neither of them wanted to let go, but of course they knew they would have to. Eventually.

CHAPTER 5

Back at school, Riley and Maya headed into their new history class, clutching the tiny green papers that equaled their freedom from Mr. Matthews.

"Transfer slip! Boom!" Riley announced, plunking the paper down on the teacher's desk.

"And boom!" Maya said, following suit.

"Greetings, new classmates!" Riley shouted as she waved at the roomful of gloriously unfamiliar students. "Riley Matthews, ready to be your friend!"

"'Sup," Maya added. "I'm Maya. Ya don't look me in the eyes."

The teacher, who looked like a female version of

Mr. Matthews, with her long dark curls and navy-blue suit, stared impatiently at Riley and Maya. "You two are late. You two don't talk. You two sit there and there." She waved Riley and Maya to empty seats on either side of the classroom.

"There and *there*?" Riley couldn't possibly fathom the vast distance between the two desks.

"No, no," Maya told the teacher. "We sit together."

"In the middle of everything," Riley explained. Surely this teacher would understand.

But alas, she was having none of it. "Move!" the teacher barked at them, as though she was leading an army instead of eighth-grade history.

"Eek!" Maya screamed, uncharacteristically frightened.

"Bye-bye," Riley said glumly, throwing her arms around her best friend.

"Excuse me, were you two trying to have a moment?" the teacher asked in a softer voice, gently pulling Riley and Maya apart.

Maya nodded.

"You two don't get a moment!" the teacher informed them, back in drill sergeant mode. "This is not *The You Two Show*."

"We were told it was," Riley said, pouting and giving Maya's hand one last squeeze before they slunk over to their desks.

On the way, Riley and Maya looked down at the two girls seated in the front row where they would normally be. Their new classmates weren't nearly as unfamiliar as Riley had initially thought. The girl in Riley's spot had long dark hair and even a pink shirt that looked kind of like Riley's, and the girl in Maya's spot had long blond hair and a green army jacket over a bright yellow T-shirt that looked kind of like Maya's. Even the boys who were seated where Lucas and Farkle would have been looked like cheap knockoffs of their friends—a similar checkered shirt and dark blond hair for Lucas, a turtleneck and helmetlike auburn hair for Farkle.

What is this? Riley wondered. *Some sort of alternate universe?*

Riley and Maya tried to settle into their new seats, but they were too far away from each other. It didn't feel right. *At all.* Riley tried to lean into the middle of the classroom, far enough to get close to Maya. But there was no way. There were too many desks and students between them. Maya did the same. But it was hopeless! At long last, Riley and Maya leapt into the laps of the students seated in the two middle desks. Much better. Much closer.

The teacher, who had been observing the entire thing, slammed a book down on her desk, scaring Riley and Maya right back into their own seats.

Then she launched into her lesson. "During the gold rush, people left the comfort of their own surroundings in the hope of finding greater riches in an inhospitable land, far from the ones they loved," the teacher began lecturing the class.

"Excuse me," Riley interrupted, rising to her feet.

"I will not warn you again, side person!" the teacher yelled.

Appalled, Riley sank back into her chair.

"You tell her, Mom!" the girl in the front row—the Riley knockoff—said to the teacher.

Wait. Knockoff Riley was the *daughter* of the knockoff female version of Mr. Matthews? Things were getting seriously weird.

"You . . . failed me," Knockoff Maya said to Female Knockoff Mr. Matthews, holding up a paper with a big red *F* written on it.

"Ha!" sneered Knockoff Farkle.

"I saw a goat give birth," said Knockoff Lucas to Knockoff Riley. He even had a southern drawl like Lucas!

"Hi," said Knockoff Riley shyly to Knockoff Lucas.

"Hey," said Knockoff Lucas.

What the heck? We really are *in some sort of alternate universe,* Riley thought.

"Waitaminute!" Real Maya suddenly exploded, leaping up from her desk, clearly on the same page as Real Riley.

"Students number six and seven," fumed Female Knockoff Mr. Matthews, looking from Real Maya to Real Riley.

"That's *us*?" Riley asked, glancing at Maya.

"I believe so," Maya replied.

"Students number six and seven?" Riley was horrified.

"Hey, at least she's talking to us," Maya offered.

"Yesss?" Riley batted her lashes at Female Knockoff Mr. Matthews.

"Get out!" the teacher bellowed, pointing to the door.

"Fine," Riley replied as she stomped over to Maya and put her arm around her best friend. "Well, at least we get a dramatic exit!"

The girls tossed their hair and waltzed out with as much dramatic flair as possible. Alas, nobody seemed to be paying attention to them. That really hammered home just how alternate this universe was—a universe where Riley and Maya didn't seem to matter at all—and Riley could feel her world crashing down, down, down.

CHAPTER 6

Once again, Riley seemed to be floating out in space. This time she was near the moon, with the earth far behind her, distant and small.

"Here's what's funny," Riley said. "If you're standing on the moon, you'd think the earth was revolving around you, instead of the other way around. It's really all about perspective." Suddenly, the earth spun right by her. It was enormous. Then the other planets spun by, one by one. Then the sun came along, and the earth looked like a tiny speck by comparison. All at once, Riley could see the entire galaxy—and then other galaxies—and she almost couldn't see the earth, or really anything, at all. "It's hard not to believe you're the center of everything," Riley observed. "Until something shows you you're not."

Even without Riley and Maya there, Mr. Matthews was determined to continue teaching his history class.

"*Our Town* by Thornton Wilder," he said, holding up a small book. "My favorite play."

"You can't teach English!" Farkle complained.

"It's all about the history—" Mr. Matthews continued.

"There ya go," Lucas said, smiling at the teacher.

"—of people just like you and me," Mr. Matthews said. "Mostly about not taking what we have for granted. And a girl who gets a chance to take one look at the life she left behind."

As Mr. Matthews opened the book, preparing to read an excerpt, Riley and Maya snuck in through the door. They placed their transfer slips on the teacher's desk and crept into the chairs at their usual desks in the front row.

"'Just for a moment now we're all together,'" Mr. Matthews read purposefully, without acknowledging that the girls had returned. "'Just for a moment we're happy. Let's really look at one another.'"

Mr. Matthews glanced up from the book and took notice of Riley and Maya, in their seats, hands folded like model students. The girls, like many of the other students in the class, exchanged meaningful looks, acknowledging each other.

"Well, hello, girls," Mr. Matthews said. "You're back?"

"Yesss." Maya widened her eyes and forced a tight smile, clearly trying not to show the defeat on her face.

"As bad as this is . . ." Riley began.

"Everything else is worse," Maya concluded.

"Well, welcome back, ladies." Mr. Matthews

smiled. "You're just in time for today's lesson."

"Did we miss anything?" Riley was suddenly concerned.

"Nah, we're just putting everything back in place. The real lesson begins right"—Mr. Matthews paused for a moment, then snapped his fingers—"now."

Riley still had no idea what "real lesson" her dad had been talking about as she and Maya entered Svorski's Bakery, their favorite after-school hangout. "Face it," Riley said to Maya. "There's no escaping him."

"He's everywhere," Maya agreed. "How we gonna rule the school if everywhere we go . . ."

"We run right into my"—Riley turned around and bumped straight into Mrs. Matthews—"mother? Mom! What are you doing here?"

"Is *my*-krainian bakery," Mrs. Matthews told her, and then spun around to look at Auggie with big, expectant eyes.

"Still not funny," Auggie said from the table where he was sitting with Mrs. Svorski.

"Not funny?" Mrs. Matthews frowned, defeated, as she looked at Auggie and Mrs. Svorski. "I'll tell you what's not funny. This place loses a dollar fifty on every *bulochki*."

"I bake with love," Mrs. Svorski explained, setting her teacup down on its saucer. "How can you put price on love?"

"Awww . . . *watch me!*" Mrs. Matthews replied, jabbing a price pin into the big sweet bakery bun on the table in front of Auggie. "Four ninety-five!"

"Oooh, *ka-ching!*" Mrs. Svorski smiled, impressed.

"Bakery window!" Riley whispered loudly to Maya, narrowing her eyes and pointing to the large cozy seat by the door. "Bakery window right now!"

Maya laughed as she followed her best friend and plopped down on the giant old cushion. "That's nice," Maya said, continuing to giggle awkwardly.

"Your dad's at our school, your mom's at our hangout. That's nice."

"You're laughing at me?" Riley demanded.

"Inside I'm crying so hard," Maya explained.

As the girls continued to despair, Mrs. Svorski handed a metal container to Riley's little brother. "Auggie, this is for you," said the old woman. "Is flour shaker. From Ukraine. Antique. Like me. You take now. You are little baker."

"What should I do with it?" Auggie, wide-eyed, asked in wonder.

"Keep safe," Mrs. Svorski told him. "Treasure always. Very important what's in there."

"Thanks, Mrs. Svorski!" Auggie could not have been more excited.

"Thank you, Mrs. Svorski," echoed Mrs. Matthews, deeply touched by the exchange.

"Oh, thank *you*, Topanga," Mrs. Svorksi said, running a hand along Mrs. Matthews's long brown hair before turning to pat the little boy on his chin. "And Auggie."

In the window seat, Riley still couldn't get over the complete disaster her life had become. "I can't escape them, Maya! My parents are constantly circling me. Like planets."

Just then, two giant hands and a face appeared in the window above Riley's head. "Hello!" Mr. Matthews smiled before bounding into the bakery like an eager, happy puppy. He pulled Riley up out of the window seat and gave her a big hug. "Riley, I haven't seen you for twenty minutes. Did you miss me? 'Cause I missed you!"

Mr. Matthews looked over and grabbed Auggie by the hand, pulling him into a group hug. "Auggie, come here. I missed you, too, bud."

While her family enjoyed their afternoon reunion, Mrs. Matthews got back to bakery business. "Mrs. Svorski, I have someone who I think could be a perfect manager for the bakery when I can't be here."

"This person knows way around food game?" Mrs. Svorski asked, looking unsure.

"Absolutely. She's also very colorful. She really gets into whatever she's doing."

"Sounds like good woman."

As they both turned to look toward the door, in walked Katy Hart, Maya's mom. She was not only a waitress but an actress—and, wearing an old-country housecoat and apron and a tattered pink kerchief in her messy blond hair, she was ready to play her new role to the hilt.

"Sorry I'm late," Mrs. Hart said in her best eastern European accent, leaning dramatically against the doorpost. "My donkey died on way here. Ahhh!" she continued, walking into the bakery and inhaling deeply. "Smells like being back in kitchen in Ukraine, waiting for Tato to come home, hoping he has not lost last finger in field mower." She paused for effect and then, eyes downcast, concluded, "Oh, no. He did."

Maya watched her mother's performance, dumbfounded. Could this really be happening?

But not everyone was unhappy about Mrs. Hart's presence.

"Poor Tato," Mrs. Svorski empathized. "He can never win at paper, rock, scissors. You always know rock is coming."

Mrs. Hart nodded as she and Mrs. Svorski looked deep into each other's eyes and then, pounding their fists, chanted in unison, "One, two, three—rock!"

As they knocked their fists together, Mrs. Svorski turned to Mrs. Matthews and said, "Oh, I like her."

Satisfied that the performance was just about over, Maya dragged herself out of the window seat and over to Mrs. Hart. "Mom," she said.

"Oh, Mayabushka!" Mrs. Hart smiled before dropping the accent and returning to her usual self. She rushed to Maya and, embracing her, said, "I'm gonna be here all the time now, baby girl! How great is that?"

Maya was almost too pained to look at Riley,

but she tried. Her best friend returned the look of complete agony. With these new developments, it was pretty much official: the best year ever had turned into the worst year ever.

CHAPTER 7

Maya and Riley straightened themselves up and prepared for a difficult, but necessary, conversation with their parents.

"Mom," Maya began, "you can't be here."

"Dad, Mom, you're everywhere," Riley chimed in, looking at her parents.

"We just need some space," Maya explained.

"It's like you're circling around us," Riley added.

Mr. and Mrs. Matthews's faces clouded over with confusion. "I'm sorry," Mr. Matthews said. "You think *we're* circling around *you*?"

"Yes." Riley nodded.

"Oh, I see." Mrs. Matthews smirked as she

turned to Mr. Matthews. "So, I guess we're all done with parenting?"

"Yes, it seems we're all done with that part now!" Mr. Matthews grabbed his wife's hand and pumped it up and down. "Good job, Topanga!"

"Good job, Cory!" Mrs. Matthews laughed. "Remember that whole potty training thing that we did for her? And now she wants to leave. . . ."

"Oh, I loved every minute of that. Good times!" Mr. Matthews shook his head and chuckled as they reminisced.

"So, you're okay with this?" Riley wasn't entirely convinced.

"Oh, yeah, we understand," Mrs. Matthews assured her. "You're a grown-up. You know everything there is to know."

"Yup, you're ready to move away," Mr. Matthews agreed.

Wait. What?

"Well, I mean, I'd like to stay in my old bedroom. . . ." Riley wasn't sure this was headed in *exactly* the direction she'd intended.

"Okay, you'll just drop us a line when you get married and have kids?" Mrs. Matthews asked.

"Mom, I just don't want you to be *everywhere*."

"Okay, well, when you need us, we'll be at home," Mrs. Matthews assured Riley as Mr. Matthews held up his hands and backed away.

"And I'll be back there," Mrs. Hart said to Maya, motioning behind the counter of the bakery, "staying out of your way."

"Okay." Maya shrugged.

"Good. So nobody feels bad about this," Riley said, attempting to get a bit more clarification on the matter.

"Well, let's see what happens," Mr. Matthews said with a quick smile.

Riley wasn't totally sure she should accept that, but what else could she do? As she and Maya went and sat down in a booth, Mrs. Svorski went to the counter to talk to Mrs. Hart. "So, you here now?" she asked her.

"I'm here now." Mrs. Hart smiled.

"Good." Mrs. Svorski nodded. Then she turned

around to give Auggie an affectionate pinch on the cheek.

"Ready?" Mrs. Matthews asked Auggie, taking him by the hand. He nodded, picking up the flour shaker Mrs. Svorski had given to him, before glancing around the bakery and heading to the door with his parents. As they made their way out, they paused and looked back inside at Mrs. Svorski, who was wandering around and gazing at the pictures, so full of history—*her* history—hanging on the walls.

"So," Riley said to Maya as they sat in the booth.

"Here we are," Maya replied with a smile.

"Kings," Riley said.

But somehow, she wasn't feeling very regal.

CHAPTER 8

Riley stood in front of an image of the earth slowly rotating.

"The sun doesn't go around the earth," Riley said. "We're the ones moving. We orbit the sun. Because we need it. We need its light and its heat. And if it wasn't there, we'd be dark and alone."

Just then, the images behind Riley faded to black. She stepped away from the screen where she had been speaking—where she had, in fact, been giving a eulogy—and walked to an easel, where a large photograph of a smiling Mrs. Svorski perched.

"I wasn't in Mrs. Svorski's orbit for very long," Riley said to the roomful of friends and loved ones who were gathered in the bakery, "and I missed out on someone wonderful. My brother knew better. He was her very good friend."

Riley looked at Auggie, who sat at a table in his little gray suit, devastated, clutching the flour shaker Mrs. Svorski had given him. Riley's parents stood behind Auggie, trying to hold it together. Riley walked to Maya, who was seated at a table with Mrs. Hart, Lucas, and Farkle, and brought her to the front of the room, where Riley had been speaking.

"We think that we're the center of the universe," Riley said, still clutching Maya's hand, as the screen behind them lit up again with images of the heavens. "But the truth is we need to circle the ones we love for as long as they're here."

At that, Maya stepped away from Riley, walked to Mrs. Hart, and hugged her mother harder than she ever had in her life. Following her best friend's lead, Riley walked to her parents and Auggie and circled her arms around them.

"We need to hold them close, because no matter how far we travel, they are the ones who hold us in place. It's gravity. Without it, we would all just float away from each other," Riley said before walking back up to the screen, which flashed images of New York City, followed by Earth and the solar system, more galaxies, and the vastness of the universe.

"We're not kings at all. Just tiny little specks. My name is Riley Matthews. From New York City, the United States of America, continent of North America, Western Hemisphere, Earth, the solar system, the universe. The mind of God. That's from *Our Town*. My father's favorite play." Riley looked at her father, who beamed with pride. "Just for a moment we're all together," Riley continued. "Let's *really* look at one another." She gazed out at her family, who looked back at her. Maya looked up at her mother, who stared down lovingly at her, stroking her hair.

"Good night, Mrs. Svorski," Riley said, looking fondly at the photograph one last time.

As Mr. and Mrs. Matthews stared into each other's eyes, Riley walked to Auggie, picked him up, and sat him on her lap, hugging him tightly.

"Good job, Riley," Auggie told her.

"I know you're gonna miss her, buddy," Riley replied.

"She gave me her flour shaker," Auggie said, holding up the metal canister and handing it to his big sister.

"That's really nice," Riley said, admiring the gift and giving it a shake. "What's inside?" Pulling out a piece of paper, Riley said, "It's a note. Maybe she wrote you a note."

Auggie looked down at the slip of paper and could almost hear Mrs. Svorski's voice in his head as he read the words: "'It's not *my*-krainian bakery. I'm dead!'"

Auggie was horrified at first, but then he couldn't help laughing. He knew that was the reaction that would have made Mrs. Svorski happy. Then, suddenly, everyone around him started laughing, too. A bakery filled with laughter. Mrs. Svorski would have *really* loved that.

Auggie turned to look up at Mr. and Mrs. Matthews. "I love you guys," he said softly, and they all hugged each other.

Back at the apartment, everyone but Mr. Matthews was asleep. He walked into the living room, where moonlight streamed in through the windows, and sat down on the couch, scrolling through the numbers on his phone until he found the one he was looking for.

"Hello, Mr. Matthews," came the weary old voice on the other end of the line after a couple of rings.

"Hey, Mr. Feeny. You doing okay?"

"Yes, Cory," the longtime teacher from his childhood replied. "I'm still here."

"Great," Mr. Matthews said with a smile. "That's great."

Knowing that Mr. Feeny was still around was all it took to give him a bit of peace—to reassure him that, for all the ways in which his world was still changing, in which his *family's* world was changing, there were parts of it that hadn't. Not completely, anyway.

Walking to school barefoot? Nightmare.
Seeing Lucas outside class? DREAMY...;-)

BELGIUM 1831

Almost afraid to see who will be teaching our
eighth-grade class.

Note to self:
If your new teacher
tells you to take a
seat, he doesn't
mean ON his desk.
Oops!

Another note to self:
Do not touch your
teacher on the nose—
no matter how happy
you are to see him.

Can't believe Maya told my dad, "Buy yourself something pretty." She's my hero.

Auggie at Mrs. Svorski's bakery. Gotta love that kid.

A death is sad, but it reminds you how important the people you love are.

Right after I say
nothing's gonna
change my world,
Zay shows up.
Hmmm . . .

Apparently, Zay and Lucas know each other. :-O

Zay is saying that Lucas is a year older and has a shady past. Whaaaat?!?

This is Auggie trying to out-tantrum me. Nice try, kid.

Zay is not as tough as he pretends to be.

Luckily, Lucas is! And did I mention he's cute, too? *Sigh.* ♡

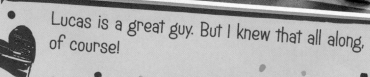
Lucas is a great guy. But I knew that all along, of course!

CHAPTER 1

Riley and Maya stood at their lockers. It was a brand-new day of an *almost* brand-new school year, and Riley was feeling good. Finally.

"Y'know what I like?" Riley asked Maya as she slammed her locker door, then quickly snapped her fingers. "Life! And I like it when it doesn't change. We should sing our happy song."

"We don't have a happy song," Maya pointed out, furrowing her brow.

"We should have a happy song!" Riley replied as they made their way to first period.

"We will *never* have a happy song," Maya fired back firmly.

"Not with that attitude," Riley noted, ever the yin to Maya's yang. Or was it yang to Maya's yin? The details didn't really matter. The point was that they balanced each other out. It was one of the many things Riley loved about their best friendship. It was something she could count on—and she liked being able to count on things.

"So you don't want anything to change?" Maya asked as they walked into history class and headed for their desks.

"Nooo," Riley confirmed, sitting down. "Don't like change. Change fills my pockets with pennies of uncertainty."

As Maya shot yet another puzzled look in Riley's direction, their classmates settled into their seats and Mr. Matthews began talking to the class. "All right, so, shall we actually, finally learn about what happened in Belgium in 1831?"

"No!" Farkle barked defiantly.

"No?" Mr. Matthews asked, dumbfounded. It *was* a little odd. Farkle was *always* ready to learn.

"I always get my hopes up and then something happens to hurt my little Farkle heart," the ginger-haired boy, clad in one of his trademark turtlenecks—this one green—under an orange-and-blue-striped rugby shirt, explained. "Well, this time I refuse to believe."

"In 1831 . . ." Mr. Matthews began in a tantalizing voice, clearly trying to coax Farkle out of his cynical shell.

"Yeeesss?" It sure didn't take much to reel Farkle back in. "Wait!" he said to Riley when she turned to look at him. "Anything suddenly going to happen to you?"

"No changes. Lovin' life," Riley insisted.

"Anything going to happen to you?" Farkle asked, turning to Lucas.

"Nothing ever happens to me," Lucas replied.

"Maya?" Farkle asked, turning to look at Maya. But she was crashed out, head on desk, actually snoring. Seeing her asleep, Farkle shivered, a bit too riled up with excitement. "Omigosh! This is it!"

Unfazed, Mr. Matthews returned to his lesson. "In 1831, Belgium—"

But before he could go any further, yet again he was interrupted—this time by a new student walking through the door.

"What?" the boy asked as he marched into the room, puffing up his chest with confidence. "Y'all started without me?"

"Get out!" Farkle growled, jumping to his feet. His eyes widened like he'd been possessed, his voice so loud and angry that even Maya woke up and turned her attention toward the new student.

"Somebody in this room is going to be very surprised to see me," said the boy. He had a mesmerizing smile and dark skin that practically glowed against his aqua-blue-and-yellow plaid shirt.

"Is it me?" Riley asked, captivated.

"No, sugar, but could you *be* any cuter?" the boy replied, his dark eyes locking with hers.

"Well, I can't answer that," Riley managed to

respond, even though the boy's extreme charm was making her feel a little dizzy.

"You got a transcript, kid?" Mr. Matthews interrupted the moment.

"Yeah, I do," said the boy, handing a manila folder to Riley's dad. "And hey, check out them grades. Here, let me sing them to you." He got into position, like he was about to audition for a singing competition, and then sang out, "De de de de de, de—*ef*."

"Yeah, I know that song," Maya said with a smile.

"'Isaiah Babineaux,'" Mr. Matthews read from the paper in the folder. "From Austin, Texas."

Wait a second. Austin, Texas? Riley thought. Was it possible that this new guy and Lucas *knew* each other? Riley, along with every other student, turned to look at Lucas, obviously putting the same Austin-plus-Austin equation together—and the answer, based on the look of frustration on Lucas's face, was a clear yes.

"What are you doing here, Zay?" Lucas asked glumly.

"Well, the first thing I'm doin' is waitin' for a better reaction from you."

"Maya, something's changing," Riley muttered to her best friend, not liking the direction things appeared to be taking.

"Okay, Mr. Teach, where do I sit?" Isaiah asked, leaning against Mr. Matthews's desk, scoping out the classroom. "You know, usually I'm more of a back-row kind of guy."

Back-row Brenda, peering at the new guy through her giant red-framed glasses, looked like she might explode with excitement as she waved enthusiastically in his direction.

"Whoa." Isaiah squinted at Brenda, examining her more closely. "That's unusual."

"Have a seat right there, Mr. Babineaux," Mr. Matthews said, motioning to the desk behind Lucas.

Riley turned. "Lucas, you know this Isaiah?" she inquired.

"Yeah, tell 'em—you know me good," Isaiah said, sitting on top of his desk instead of in the seat.

"How 'bout we talk *later*, okay?" Lucas replied, clearly not in the mood to explain their relationship to anyone—then or perhaps ever.

Isaiah, or "Zay," got the message, raising his hands in defeat and backing off.

"Well, Mr. Babineaux, if you work out as well as last year's new student," Mr. Matthews said, motioning to Lucas, "we're happy to have you."

"Wait, what?" Zay seemed surprised. "Lucas, you're doing okay here?"

"Why *wouldn't* he be doing okay here?" Riley asked.

"Not currently on probation?" Zay continued his line of questioning. "No disciplinary action? They just let you wander free?"

What is he talking about? Riley thought. *Lucas? Disciplinary action? Does Zay have Lucas mixed up with someone else?*

"Sit down!" Farkle growled in the same demon-crazed voice he'd used earlier, which was terrifying enough that Zay finally retreated to his seat. Eager to seize the moment, Farkle turned to Mr. Matthews and, in a calm and happy voice, added, "Okay. New guy's all settled in and there's still class time left. So *do* it! Do it while I'm still tingly!"

"So," Mr. Matthews said, laughing, as he followed Farkle's direction, "in 1831, Belgium declared its—"

But yet again, he was interrupted. This time it was Yogi, their quiet little classmate who *never* said anything. "What is the secret of life?" Yogi asked.

Everyone turned to glare at Yogi, Farkle especially. "I'm sorry, Mr. Farkle," the dark-haired boy said with a soft smile, closing his eyes and clenching his fists intently before rising to his feet, opening his eyes, and addressing Mr. Matthews. "I know I am not your daughter, but I, too, have value in this world. What is the secret of life?"

Sighing, Mr. Matthews looked at Farkle and flung up his hands in defeat. Laughing apologetically, he grabbed the eraser from the chalkboard and headed for the large letters spelling out BELGIUM, 1831.

"Don't do it!" Farkle half begged, half commanded Mr. Matthews, who stopped and turned to look at Farkle. "Put that eraser down and nobody gets hurt!"

But Mr. Matthews took eraser to board. Just like that, the day's lesson—and all hope of the class's avoiding change—disappeared.

"HUWAAAUUUUUUUGGGGGHHHHH!" Farkle screamed a possessed scream, pulling his rugby shirt up to hide his entire head, which he then slammed on the desk.

Wow. Guess I'm not the only one around here who doesn't like change, Riley thought.

"Yogi has asked the primary riddle of the universe," Mr. Matthews told the class. "What is the secret of life? People spend their whole lives trying to figure it out. I was lucky. I had a teacher who cared enough about me to make sure I knew. Lucas. You got an opinion on this?"

"Yeah, whaddya got, Mr. Moral Compass?" Maya asked, turning in her chair to look at Lucas.

"Did you just call Lucas Friar your moral compass?" Zay asked with an incredulous laugh, slapping Lucas on the back. "Ha! They just called you moral compass!"

Lucas turned and stared Zay down until, once again, Zay retreated—this time with a soft "okay."

"Something bad is happening, Maya," Riley whispered to her best friend. But Maya seemed more intrigued than upset.

"Yeah, it occurs to me you're trying to tell us Ranger Rick was a little different back in Texas," Maya said to Zay.

"A *little*?" Zay replied, then addressed Lucas. "What do they know exactly? 'Cause I wouldn't wanna say anything wrong. They know you're a year older, right?"

"Yeah, now they do," Lucas said awkwardly, turning around to glare at Zay.

"Oh, yeah, it's *my* fault," Zay replied—and then,

as if it should already have been obvious to everyone there, he added, "*Look* at ya!"

Wait. What? It can't be true. Can it? Lucas—a year older than the rest of us? A year older than me? Riley thought.

"Okay, that's enough, Mr. Babineaux," Mr. Matthews said.

"Oh, so you know about him?" Zay asked the teacher.

"I know all about Mr. Friar," Mr. Matthews replied, his voice soft and sad.

There's no way this is happening. Not only is Lucas a year older than us—than me—*but my dad already knows something else about him?* Riley's palms were sweating; her heart was racing. She was sure she was going to pass out at any second.

"Excuse me?" Riley finally managed to say, turning to stare at her father.

"Riley, you're shaking," Maya said, but Riley needed to focus on her dad, to find out *exactly* what he'd heard—and kept from her.

"Dad, you know something?"

Before her father could answer, Lucas spoke up. "Back in Texas—"

"Lucas, you sure?" Mr. Matthews asked softly while Zay smiled a self-satisfied smile. Lucas nodded.

"Back in Texas, I did something. I had to leave."

Nooooo! No, no, no, no, no. Lucas was perfect. He was sweet and kind and a good friend to everyone. What could he possibly have done that was so awful?

"It was *great*!" Zay chimed in. "I mean, they threw him out of the whole school!"

"What?" Riley demanded.

"I came here to get a new start," Lucas explained to her. "Nobody knew me here."

He could say *that* again!

"I know him," Zay said, raising his hand and grinning from ear to ear.

"Do *I* know you?" Riley asked softly.

But she wasn't sure she wanted to hear the answer. It was as if everything Lucas had been, everything she wanted him to be, had been erased as easily as "BELGIUM, 1831" on the chalkboard. He had been changed into something else, like pennies of uncertainty she didn't want or need. Just like that, she wasn't liking life—especially its *secrets*—at all. And Maya was right: they definitely didn't have a happy song.

CHAPTER 2

By the time the lunch bell rang, Riley was feeling better. She had decided there was no possible way Lucas was the guy Zay had suggested he was. She knew Lucas. He was the guy she and her friends had known for the past year. The New York Lucas. Nobody's words—especially words from someone Lucas knew before—could change that. Because if those words were true, that would make Lucas a . . . No, she couldn't even think it.

"We don't know the story yet," Maya said between bites of salad, clearly unaware that Riley had already figured out the whole thing. "Let's know the story before you go to Rileytown."

"I'm not going to Rileytown. I'm calm."

"I like it worse when you're calm," Maya complained. "Come on, be you!"

Maya grabbed Riley's arms, lifted them up, and made them flail all around her head as she did her best Riley impression, complete with an enthusiastic "Yyyyyyyaaaaaaayyyyyyy!"

Riley had to laugh when pieces of food flew off the fork that was still in her hand. But then up walked Lucas, and she grew serious. "Deny it," she told him with a kind but determined smile as he sat down at the table.

"Riley—" Lucas said.

"Tell me whoever this Zay kid is, he can't just come in here and change you from the Lucas we know," she continued, reciting the instructions she'd been practicing in her head since first period. "Tell me nothing changes."

"That's all you have to do, Lucas," Maya chimed in, backing up Riley, as she almost always did. "You hear me? I just called you by your actual name for the first time ever. That's how important this is to me. Because it's important to her." Maya paused for a moment, placing a hand gently on Riley's shoulder, and then urgently whispered, "Deny it."

Lucas shook his head and simply said, "I can't."

Who knew those two little words could bring Riley's whole world crashing down? She sat there for a moment, trying to wrap her head around what Lucas had just revealed.

"I like you," Riley finally told him, determined to be as honest as she'd ever been in her whole life. Something he, apparently, hadn't been. "I went on my first date with you. Do you think it's right to let me like you without telling me who you are?"

The way he smiled when she told him she liked him nearly melted Riley's heart. *Nearly*. But relationships weren't based on smiles.

"You know who I am," Lucas insisted, his green eyes as sincere as they'd always been. "I'm Ranger Rick. We rode on a white horse. I asked your father's blessing just to go on a date with you. Who *does* that?"

He had a point—a lot of points. But what about

the stuff Zay had said? "Were you thrown out of school?" Riley asked.

"Yes."

"For a whole year?"

"Yes."

"I finally like you," Maya interjected, pointing a forkful of lettuce at him.

"You told me you wanted to be a veterinarian," Riley recounted. "You told me you gave birth to a horse."

"That had to hurt," Maya added with a slight southern drawl.

"Why didn't you tell me about this?" Riley asked plainly.

"It's not something I'm proud of," Lucas replied with a shrug. "I thought I could start over. I guess I was wrong. I guess you do something and that's the end of you."

Lucas looked so lost and alone—like his sweet, sad story could make Riley rethink the situation. But what he was saying was ridiculous. "You think *that's* what I'm upset about? Whatever you *did*?"

Riley was beside herself. She wasn't that judgmental, and Lucas of all people should know that about her. But apparently he didn't—and that broke her heart into even tinier pieces. "Then I don't know you," she said, shaking her head, tears beginning to sting her eyes. "And you don't know me."

"Why are you *acting* like this?" Lucas demanded in a raised, almost angry, voice.

"Friends talk to you and real friends listen, remember?" she explained as calmly as she could, recalling one of the very first real conversations they'd had. "I would have listened. I'm your friend. Whatever you did, why wouldn't you trust me with it? People who care about you are supposed to trust you with stuff."

As the words "people who care about you" echoed in her ears, Riley suddenly remembered the worst part of it all—the part that had made her so upset she'd decided Lucas couldn't possibly have done those things Zay had talked about. "Waitaminute," she finally said, getting up from the lunch table, searching Maya's face and then Lucas's. Not only had he done what Zay had said, but someone else had kept the truth from her, too—someone who meant the world to her. *"My* father *knew about this?"*

That's when the tears really started to burn Riley's eyes. But she wasn't going to let Lucas see her cry. So she quickly turned and stormed out of the cafeteria, as fast as she possibly could, determined not to look back. After all, looking back was what had started all of this in the first place.

CHAPTER 3

Mrs. Matthews was just sitting down on the couch with a cup of tea, ready to relax and curl up with a book after another long day in court, when her husband burst through the apartment door.

"Topanga!" he shouted, rushing to her. "There could be a significant amount of drama heading in our general direction."

"Y'know, normal people consider their home to be a sanctuary from the storm of the outside world," Mrs. Matthews replied. "Why can't we be normal people?"

"Because we have *this*—" Mr. Matthews made

a grand gesture toward the front door, eager for his wife to understand exactly what had happened at school. But nobody was there. The door remained closed. "I never get those right," Mr. Matthews said, shaking his head with disappointment. "But it's coming!"

"'Kay," Mrs. Matthews said, playing along. "What do you wanna do until it does?"

"I could throw a tantrum about absolutely nothin' for ya," Auggie offered from his spot at the kitchen table, ever the dutiful son. "Watch me."

Auggie jumped onto the table, stretched out on his belly, and banged his fists and feet. *Why don't we have any*"—the curly-haired boy paused and appeared to be struggling to come up with something really important—"*jelly?*" he finally demanded.

"There's some in the fridge," Mrs. Matthews replied calmly.

"*Well . . . I don't like that kind of jelly!*" Auggie

insisted, pounding his fists and feet even harder.

Then, finally, the real storm arrived in the form of Riley.

"You *knew*!" she shouted at her father as she stomped into the apartment and slammed the door behind her.

"Well, I'm not gonna beat *that*," Auggie observed, climbing down from the table and watching his sister take over.

"Boy, are you gonna get yelled at, Matthews!" said Maya as she rushed in through the apartment door before realizing Riley was already there. She turned her attention to her best friend. "Oh, I already missed it? Do it again."

"A normal-people sanctuary," Mrs. Matthews sighed. "I'd like a fountain. Maybe a candle."

"How could you keep something like this away from me?" Riley screamed at her father.

"Just someplace where people don't get hysterical over every little thing," Mrs. Matthews continued to muse.

"Yes, I did know that Lucas was expelled," Mr. Matthews told his daughter with a shrug, as if it were no big deal.

"*What?*" Mrs. Matthews demanded, abandoning her serene fantasy.

Mr. Matthews turned and whispered to his wife, "Topanga, you knew this. I told you all about this."

"Yeah, I know you told me all about this, but I want nothing to do with *that*," Mrs. Matthews explained in hushed confidence as she shot a glance at Riley, who was glaring at her father, clearly angrier with him than she'd ever been in her life.

"Why would you let me like him if you know something about him?" Riley demanded.

"Riley, honey," Mrs. Matthews said carefully, "whatever this is about Lucas—that I know nothing about—I'm sure your father knows exactly what you need to learn from it."

"Really?" Riley widened her eyes, hopeful

yet skeptical, shaking her head. "Dad? You got anything?"

But her father stood in silence. For once, he seemed to be all out of lessons. For once, he was speechless.

CHAPTER 4

It was a new day, and Riley had no interest in being in history class. History had officially become her least favorite subject ever.

"Al washes a car in six minutes," Mr. Matthews said to the students. "Fred washes the same car in eight minutes. How long does it take Al and Fred to wash the same car together?"

Wait. Was that his plan? To turn history into math?

"How is this anything?" Riley asked.

"Three minutes, twenty-five point seven seconds," Farkle offered, looking up from the paper where he had been feverishly working on the equation.

"Wrong," Mr. Matthews said flatly.

"I'm sorry, what'd you just say?" Farkle demanded.

"You're wrong," Mr. Matthews repeated.

"*I'm* wrong?" Farkle fumed. "You're a history teacher teaching English, science, whatever you got going on at home." Farkle paused for effect, then offered an example to illustrate his point: "You waltz your wife in here on career day—"

"She's a respected attorney," Mr. Matthews insisted, like it was the most logical thing in the world.

"My father says she should've been my mother!" Farkle hissed at the teacher.

Mr. Matthews sighed, exhausted and defeated. "Whaddaya want from me?"

"Mr. Matthews teaches us about a lot of things," Lucas chimed in, coming to the teacher's defense as he shot a critical look at Riley. "*He's* open-minded that way."

"He can *be* open-minded, because *he* knows who we are," Riley fired back.

"Oooh." Lucas smiled slyly at Mr. Matthews. "She took us *both* out."

"I teach this way because in my old school I had a very strict teacher," Mr. Matthews explained.

"He teach history, English, or math?" Zay asked.

"I don't know," Mr. Matthews said, clearly still a bit puzzled by that one himself all those years later. "But in his class there was no talking. No interruptions."

"So you didn't like him?" Zay asked.

"I *loved* him," Mr. Matthews insisted.

"Then why don't you teach like him?" Farkle asked.

"Because I would never try to be like him," Mr. Matthews explained. "I could only fail. I only succeed with you guys if I get my teaching across as effectively as he did."

"You do," Maya told Mr. Matthews, and then turned to look at Zay. "He does."

"Thank you, Maya." Mr. Matthews seemed

genuinely touched. "And I will, now. Al washes a car in six minutes. Fred washes the same car in eight minutes."

"See? He thinks it's math class!" Zay tossed up his hands in frustration. "Somebody stop him!" Zay turned and shook a finger at Farkle. "You, what's your name?"

"Farkle."

"What'd you call me?" Zay scrunched up his face, disgusted.

"My name is Farkle," he explained, slowly.

"Who would *do* that to you?" Zay asked with a sympathetic frown.

"So your assignment today is to wash a car," Mr. Matthews said, intervening. He looked from Riley to Lucas. "Together."

"With him?" Riley demanded, pushing an angry thumb in Lucas's direction.

"*Especially* with him," Mr. Matthews concluded while Riley sulked.

"If you do it correctly, you will find the answer

is three minutes, twenty-five point seven seconds," Farkle insisted.

"If you do it correctly, you will find the secret of life." Mr. Matthews stared at the class, a sad but hopeful look in his eyes.

Riley felt just as sad, and far from hopeful. The assignment didn't make sense, and it probably never would. History plus math. Al plus Fred. Riley plus Lucas. Whatever the variables, there was no way it would add up to anything good.

CHAPTER 5

Standing in the school parking lot just outside the gym, Riley watched as Maya washed the Matthewses' car while Zay sat comfortably inside the vehicle with his hands behind his head, listening to the radio and nodding in time to the music.

"Done!" Maya finally announced.

Farkle, who was keeping track of how long it took each person to wash the car alone, immediately clicked the stopwatch that was hanging around his neck. "Amazing," Farkle marveled.

"How long?" Maya asked.

"Nineteen minutes, forty-two seconds," Farkle told her. "You are the worst car washer in this class."

"Oh," Maya groaned, tossing her soapy yellow rag on the ground. "You mean no one will ever ask me to wash a car for them?" She walked over to Riley and commanded, "Say it."

"You're a genius," Riley admitted.

"Oh, stop," Maya replied with false humility and a smile, tossing her hair.

Farkle looked down at his clipboard. "The only two who washed the car in six minutes and eight minutes exactly were Riley and—"

"*Lucas?*" Maya interrupted. "Was it Lucas? It couldn't have been Lucas. Was it Lucas?"

"Yeah, Lucas." Farkle nodded and smiled, surprising no one.

"I'm not washing a car with him," Riley insisted.

"Oh yes you are," Farkle fired back, pointing his finger in her face. "And you are washing it in three minutes, twenty-five point seven seconds, and I will go back to your father and I will say, 'HAAHHH!'" Determined and serious, Farkle glared at Riley and added, "Now pick up that hose."

"Fine." Riley picked up the hose.

"And you pick up that bucket," Farkle commanded Lucas.

"Yes, sir," Lucas replied, amused.

"And . . . go!" Farkle shouted, holding up the stopwatch.

Riley began to wash the car, as slowly and as far away from Lucas as she possibly could. She hosed off the front of the car while he used the sponge and soapy water to clean the back.

"No, no," Farkle complained. "Work together. The equation doesn't work if you don't work together."

"Riley, I could use some water over here to rinse this off," Lucas called to her.

"Oh. Water?" Riley stared at the ground and readied the hose. "You want some water?"

"Yes, please," Lucas responded, ever the polite southern gentleman—not that Riley believed that was the real him anymore.

"Oh, Huckleberry, Huckleberry . . ." Maya chuckled and shook her head. "Whatever bad, bad things you did at your old school, you are still such a Huckleberry."

"Why?" Lucas asked innocently. "You need water to rinse off—"

As Riley approached with the hose, Maya ducked, and the stream of water shot straight at Lucas. Riley sprayed him so hard that he dove over the hood of the car, desperate to escape the force of the water. Riley kept going at him, attacking him with the hose, while Zay watched from inside the bright blue Mini Cooper, amazed.

"Tell me what you did!" Riley shouted at Lucas.

"Nothing *this* bad!" Lucas said, jumping out from behind the car just long enough for Riley to spray him right in the face. He dove back behind the car.

"They threw you out of school!" Riley yelled.

"Wash the car!" Farkle shouted at both of them, marching over with his clipboard. "You're supposed to be washing the car! Why aren't you washing the car? Wash the car!"

But Riley was on a mission. She spun around and sprayed Farkle in the face.

"Okay!" Farkle quickly backed off.

"When are you gonna tell me what you did?" Riley demanded, turning back to glare at Lucas.

"Fine!" Lucas yelled back, soaked from head to toe. "You want me to tell you what I did?"

"Everything!" Riley insisted.

"Okay," Lucas said, softening his voice and talking to her like she was a wild animal as he reached out his hands and slowly approached her. "Good girl. Just give me the hose . . . and I'll tell you. Good girl."

"Fine." Riley handed the hose to Lucas.

Maya, amazed, slapped her forehead with her hand.

"Thank you," Riley said to Lucas.

"No, thank *you*," Lucas replied, taking the hose from her with an evil glint in his still beautiful green eyes.

That was when Riley realized what he had just done. "Maya!" she screamed as Lucas turned the hose on her and opened fire. She flew back against the fence from the force of the water and held on for stability. Zay continued to look on in amazement as he vacated the car and went to sit next to Maya on an overturned bucket.

"Wow," Zay said to Maya. "Yours is really something."

"She's a lotta work," Maya told him.

"What happens to her when you're home sick?" Zay asked.

"Oh, I can never get sick," Maya revealed, making Zay smile. "So, just between you and me . . . what'd Ranger Rick really do? Did he tip over a cow? Did he put eleven gallons in a ten-gallon hat?"

"I think I already said too much and he'll tell you when he wants to tell you," Zay replied.

"You were really best friends?" Maya asked.

"Oh, there were never better friends," Zay insisted, not entirely realizing what he was saying or who he was talking to.

Maya scoffed. "Oh, I think there were," she said. "And if Riley was coming from Texas, at least she'd tell me she was coming."

"Like I said, something happened," Zay told her.

Then, looking at Riley, he pointed at the spectacle she had become from the force of the water from the hose. "Your friend's a fountain."

Maya looked at her best friend. Lucas still had the hose on Riley, who was flapping her arms and hands and standing on one leg—just like, as Zay had noted, a fountain.

"*Flagghhh! Flagghhh!*" Riley screamed. "Wait a minute! Wait! Wait! Lucas! I lost my contact lens!"

Lucas finally stopped spraying as Riley dropped to the ground and began searching.

"Omigosh," Lucas said, rushing over to help. "Riley, I'm so sorry! I didn't mean to do that."

After a brief moment of searching, he stood up. "Wait a minute," Lucas said. "Since when do you wear—"

Ha! *Now* who had the upper hand? Riley had already slipped away to grab the bucket of soapy water, which she dumped all over Lucas's head. He stood up with the bucket on his head, and Riley rushed him like a bull and knocked him back onto the hood of the car, right where she wanted him.

Placing her hands on his upper arms, Riley spoke sincerely to Lucas, who still had the bucket on his head. "You were the first boy I ever liked," she told him. "That's a big deal for me. Are you worth it? Tell me and I'll believe you. I want to believe you. Are you worth it?"

From somewhere inside the bucket, a hollow but hopeful voice said, "Yes."

Riley took the bucket off Lucas's head and looked into his wet, soapy eyes. But before they could talk, Farkle raced over and got between them.

"You two have completely ruined this experiment for me!" Farkle fumed. "You are significantly over three minutes—"

"By how much?" Riley asked.

"A *day*!" Farkle yelled, ever the melodramatic one. "And you haven't even dried the car yet."

With that, Riley grabbed Farkle's feet; Lucas grabbed him under the armpits; and they set him on the hood of the car, using his backside like a towel as they swung him from side to side. It was impossible not to laugh at the whole thing. Even Farkle started to laugh along with Riley and Lucas.

"Okay, okay," Farkle told them between laughs. "I think it's dry!"

"You're a tight little group, aren't you?" Zay said to Maya.

"Yeah, we are," Maya replied happily, marching over to her friends and leaving Zay to ponder that.

"Yeah . . ." Zay nodded.

"Hey!" Maya yelled at Riley and Lucas indignantly. "Farkle's right! This is a serious assignment! Put Farkle down!"

Riley and Lucas stopped immediately and did as they were told.

"Now line up right there!" Maya commanded them. "Stand up straight! Straighter! I'm gonna show you how you do this right! Open your mouths! Open 'em!"

Riley and Lucas dutifully obeyed again, as did Farkle.

"Amateurs." Maya smiled, lifted the hose, and

turned it on all three of them, blowing them back onto the car.

After watching for a few moments, Zay got up and walked inside the gym. But Riley, Maya, Lucas, and Farkle were having too much fun to even realize he had left.

Finally, everything seemed to be falling back into place, and no matter how hard Maya sprayed the hose, there was no way she could wash the smile off Riley's face. Or off any of their faces.

CHAPTER 6

In history class the next morning, Mr. Matthews looked at his students, eager to hear the results of the car wash experiment.

"Al washes a car in six minutes. Fred washes the same car in eight minutes. How long does it take for Al and Fred to wash the same car together?" Mr. Matthews said, smiling, especially interested in one student's answer. "Farkle?"

"They were snapping towels at each other!" Farkle insisted. "I said, 'The car's not even dry yet!' They went . . ."

Farkle held up an imaginary hose and pretended

to spray it in one direction, then turned around and acted like he was getting squirted, doing his best impression of Riley getting blown backward, flapping her arms, and hanging on to the car for dear life. "'Whoa . . . she's a fountain!' *'Flagghhh! Flagghhh!'*" Farkle screamed, just like Riley had.

"So, not three minutes, twenty-five point seven seconds?" Mr. Matthews asked.

Farkle's face fell in agony. "I was *wruhh*," he said softly.

"Excuse me?" Mr. Matthews said.

"I was *wruhh*," Farkle repeated.

"Well, it takes a big man to admit when he was wruhh," Mr. Matthews said with a smirk. "There is no answer to this equation. Except on paper. Except in a math class—which this isn't."

"Is there an answer in life?" Lucas asked eagerly.

"Ah." Mr. Matthews nodded at Lucas. "And now we've arrived at the secret."

"Lucas's secret?" Riley asked.

"Bigger than that," Mr. Matthews replied.

"Riley, sometimes things come out when they're supposed to come out," Lucas told her.

"As long as you're not different than I think," Riley replied. "Because . . . I think a lot of you."

"I used to be different than I am now," Lucas acknowledged.

"What happened?" Riley asked.

"I came here." Lucas smiled and locked eyes with Riley, and she smiled back as her heart began to beat in double time. She knew that he was being honest with her—that he'd always been honest with her. Not telling her about his past wasn't his way of hiding who he'd been before. It was his way of becoming a new person—the person Riley knew. The person Riley liked.

"And there's your answer, Yogi," Mr. Matthews said to their classmate. "There's the secret of life."

Riley looked at her father, wanting to hear how he would explain it, eager for confirmation that she'd learned what he'd expected them all to learn.

"People change people," Mr. Matthews told the

class. "No matter what I teach you in here, learning from the people you care about is more important than the words on any page. That's why I let you talk in here sometimes. That's why it's interesting. Mr. Babineaux might've appreciated that, if he was here."

Hey, yeah. Where is Zay? Riley thought.

"Where's your friend, Mr. Friar?" Mr. Matthews asked, reading Riley's mind—as he had a tendency to do.

"I don't know," Lucas replied, suddenly looking irritated. "I can't always be responsible for him."

"Sure you can," Mr. Matthews told Lucas sincerely. "But maybe in a different way now."

"Look," Lucas said to Mr. Matthews. "Zay's mouth gets him in trouble. He thinks he's tougher than he is, maybe. But he's my friend, and I care about my friends. Riley, you understand that better than anyone." He turned to look at Riley, and then, out of nowhere, he raised his voice and demanded, "What was I *supposed* to do?"

Riley looked at the ground. Was this the other side of him? The side that got him into trouble in Austin? The Lucas he *used* to be?

"I'm sorry I got mad," Lucas said softly. "I'm working on it, okay?"

Riley looked from Lucas to her dad. Was there more to this secret of life—and to the secret of Lucas—than she thought? Had New York really changed him? Had *she* really changed him? And if Zay showed up again, would he somehow change Lucas back? It seemed like there were more secrets for her still to figure out—secrets she wasn't sure she could, or even wanted to, figure out.

In the hallway outside class, Joey Ricciardella was leaning against a locker, arms crossed, staring angrily off into space while Zay tried to talk to him. Zay was big, but Joey was *huge* and looked even bigger and badder with his tough-guy black jacket, slick black hair, and sideburns.

"So, I'm new here, y'know?" Zay told Joey. "Just trying to fit into what should be my crowd, y'know? Seeking out my kind of people, y'know? I'm sensing you know what I'm talking about. Look at you. *You* know what I'm talking about."

Zay gave Joey's shoulder a little slap, which Joey did *not* appreciate. He glared down at the point of contact and then furrowed his dark eyebrows at Zay.

"That's why I'm not in my extra math class," Zay explained. "'Cause right away, I knew you didn't fit in with these people, either. You know, these *car washers*. I'm gonna run with *you* now."

Zay slapped Joey on the shoulder, harder that time, and then leaned against the lockers next to him, like they were best buddies now. "You're welcome," Zay concluded.

But Joey had clearly heard enough. He turned and looked into Zay's eyes, grabbed him by the shirt, and—

"Oh, not again . . ." Zay said nervously as Joey lifted him off the ground and slammed him against the lockers.

"I'm up in the air," Zay said out loud, astonished that Joey could pick him up so high. "Luucaaaassss!"

Inside the history classroom, everyone suddenly heard someone yelling Lucas's name—and Lucas knew exactly who it was.

"Oh, not again . . ." Lucas groaned, getting up from his desk and turning to Mr. Matthews. "I'll be right back, sir."

"Lucas?" Mr. Matthews was clearly worried.

Riley was worried, too.

"I'm okay, sir," Lucas assured the teacher, moving toward the door with calm purpose.

"Lucas?" Mr. Matthews said more forcefully.

"I'm okay, sir," Lucas insisted, and Mr. Matthews nodded and waved him toward the door. Lucas turned to look at Riley, Maya, and Farkle and added with a smile, "If I manage to not come back expelled, you have all changed me."

With that, he walked out the door—and Riley couldn't help wondering if he was also walking out of her life. She didn't want history to repeat for Lucas. What if he got angry again? What if they *hadn't* changed him?

"Dad?" Riley looked at her father, desperate for some reassurance.

In response, he walked toward the back door of the classroom, following Lucas. Riley and her friends got up and trailed close behind.

In the hall, Joey still had Zay pinned up against a locker, and he looked like he was about to strangle him.

"I did it again," Zay managed to choke in Lucas's direction. "I'm sorry."

"It's okay, Zay," Lucas told his old friend with an understanding smile as Joey finally let go of him. "Get outta here."

But Joey leaned back against Zay so he couldn't go anywhere, and stared at Lucas. He smiled, like he was the one in charge, and then clucked at Zay, nodding to say he was allowed to leave. As Zay stepped aside, Joey leaned against the locker, got comfortable, and stared at Lucas some more.

"Are you kidding me?" Joey said to him in a thick Jersey accent, staring down at his giant knuckles, turning them every which way, examining them. "I had a neck in my hand. I *liked* it. I miss it. You my new neck?"

"Are you the one?" Lucas asked, undeterred, as he walked right up to Joey. "Because there's one in every school, isn't there? So in this school, you're the—"

"Yeah." Joey smiled a devilish smile. "It's me."

"Daddy?" Riley whispered to her father as they watched from the end of the bank of lockers. "Are you gonna stop this?"

"Not yet," Mr. Matthews told her, putting one arm protectively around his daughter and the other arm around Maya.

Riley looked at Lucas, who seemed to have grown another foot and at least a few more muscles. He wasn't backing down from Joey at all. There was intensity on his face she'd never seen before.

He didn't seem to care that Joey Ricciardella was pretty much the most dangerous kid in school.

"I couldn't help but notice your pointy boots," Lucas said to Joey, looking down at the spiky black leather. "Back in Texas we appreciate a nice pointy boot."

Then Lucas quickly stomped on Joey's foot and knocked him back against the lockers, getting right up in his face and grabbing his arms so he couldn't move.

"They can end a fight real quick," Lucas told Joey, low and fast, with a hard and determined look in his eyes. "Unless somebody knows how to put his heel on the soft part where all of your toes are."

"Ow." Joey winced, a confused look flashing across his face. It was probably the first time he'd ever said "ow" in his whole life.

"Now I'm sure you'd like to throw a punch," Lucas told Joey. "Except I got both your wrists. And I'm as strong as a horse. I don't even work at it. I just am."

"The way I see it, all that matters is what happens after you let go," Joey replied, unfazed.

"Yeah," Lucas said calmly, not afraid. "I know it'd be simpler to just start takin' shots at each other, but I'm gonna tell you something, and you really need to hear this. In the end, you're gonna be the one on the floor, and I'm gonna be the one who walks away."

"Ooooooo," Maya said softly—but this time, Lucas had gotten to her in an entirely different way than usual. Lucas had shown that he was the bigger person—the better person—just like Riley knew him to be.

He *had* been changed. Maybe his secret was that he'd gotten into a fight in Austin. Maybe he had done it to protect Zay then, too, because he had thought that was the only way to settle things. But he knew better now.

"He's gonna be a veterinarian," Riley said with a smile, looking proudly at Lucas.

"So I'm gonna do you a favor and let you keep

your reputation," Lucas continued as he finally let go of Joey's wrists, "and I'd like you to let me keep mine. Otherwise we're gonna be twenty and still be in middle school. You want that?"

"I *am* twenty," Joey replied before turning and walking away, leaving everyone thinking it was no *wonder* he was so big and tough!

Once Joey was gone, Zay rushed over to talk to Lucas. "So, I could've taken him, right?" Zay said with a sheepish smile.

"Sure." Lucas shook his head, trying to understand. "Why do you keep finding yourself in these situations?"

"Well, I like knowing you have my back," Zay explained, making his way over to the bench in the middle of the indoor quad. He was about to sit down, but then he moved over to make a little extra space for Lucas. When Lucas didn't approach, Zay turned and looked longingly in his direction, eyes *pleading* with him to sit down. Finally, Lucas obliged.

"So what are you doing here, Zay?" Lucas asked as he took a seat on the bench.

"Well, maybe I missed my best friend, all right?" Zay gushed, full of drama, waving his hands around for emphasis. "Maybe I had a best friend in Texas and he moved away and I missed hanging out with him and I convinced my entire family to pack up everything we own and—"

"Your dad got transferred?" Lucas interrupted with a knowing grin.

"Yeah, same as you." Zay nodded and shrugged.

"Look, I'm glad you're here, buddy," Lucas said, turning to face Zay. "But I don't wanna have to keep being the same guy you knew back in Texas."

"Yeah." Zay smiled and put an arm around Lucas, who responded by putting his arm around Zay. "I'm not so sure you are."

With that, the two old friends stood up and headed back into history class.

Riley could not have been happier about the way that had all turned out. Not only had Lucas survived; he had been brave, strong, and smart—and not angry at all. Mostly, he had made her proud—of him, of her dad, and even of herself and her friends.

"People change people," Riley said, smiling at her father, Maya, and Farkle.

"Secret of life," her dad said, smiling back.

As they followed Lucas and Zay back to class, Riley could tell that her dad was just as proud as she was of Lucas, Riley, and their friends—and, yeah, of himself.

CHAPTER 7

Later that night, Riley and her family were sitting around the dinner table. Maya was there, too. It was the perfect time for Riley and Auggie to play a little joke on their parents—to teach them a lesson about how they could change the same old boring meal into something *different*.

"I can drive Daddy crazy in eight seconds," Riley announced coyly.

"I can drive Mommy crazy in *six* seconds," Auggie fired back, accepting his sister's challenge, before launching into the question of the night: "How long does it take Auggie and Riley to drive Mommy and Daddy crazy *together*?"

"You feel like a movie?" Mr. Matthews asked his wife, paying no attention to Riley or Auggie.

"Love to," Mrs. Matthews replied, setting down her fork, getting up from the table, and tossing her napkin aside.

Mr. Matthews got up, too, and they both headed straight for the door.

"Hey!" Riley protested. This wasn't going according to plan at all.

"What?" Auggie demanded.

"You can't just get up in the middle of dinner and walk out on them before they drive you crazy," Maya added.

"We can do whatever we want," Mrs. Matthews replied with a giant smile. "See, we couldn't when we were kids. But that's why we became parents."

"Well, what do you call *that*?" Riley demanded of her father.

"Secret of life," Mr. Matthews replied with a sly smile.

Riley looked at Maya, who looked back at Riley, who looked at Auggie. It was so annoying. Her dad had done it again. He had taught *Riley* a lesson when she was trying to teach *him* one!

"There's lots of 'em," Mr. Matthews finally added.

As their parents each put an arm around the other and walked out of the apartment, Auggie seemed to think it was the funniest thing ever. Riley did not. How could she? Not only had they left right when she and Auggie were supposed to launch their *crazy dinner* plan; but they had abandoned their own kids—the very kids who were responsible for changing them, for turning them into parents. Parents who could do whatever they wanted!

Of course, Riley knew they wouldn't be gone long. There were still a whole lot of life secrets she had yet to learn, but this was one she'd figured out a long time before: the people who loved you—the ones who really, truly loved you—always came back. No matter how much her world might change, it was one thing Riley knew she could always count on.